Samuel Narh grew up in Ghana, West Africa. As a young child, he tended a garden, and he had a passion for watching plants grow and bear fruits. He admired the beauty of nature. He also had a habit of saving money in a wooden piggy bank. He desires to share these habits, which are being lost nowadays, with children all over the world.

_LLE
OF
PORTUANA

SAMUEL NARH

AUSTIN MACAULEY PUBLISHERS™
LONDON ∗ CAMBRIDGE ∗ NEW YORK ∗ SHARJAH

Copyright © Samuel Narh (2019)

Ordering Information:
Quantity sales: special discounts are available on quantity purchases by corporations, associations, and others. For details, contact the publisher at the address below.

Publisher's Cataloging-in-Publication data
Narh, Samuel
Elle of Portuana

ISBN 9781641824675 (Paperback)
ISBN 9781641824682 (Hardback)
ISBN 9781645364351 (ePub e-book)

Library of Congress Control Number: 2019907907

www.austinmacauley.com/us

First Published (2019)
Austin Macauley Publishers LLC
40 Wall Street, 28th Floor
New York, NY 10005
USA
mail-usa@austinmacauley.com
+1 (646) 5125767

Dedications

I dedicate this book to my four-year-old daughter, Merrit. Thank you for being my muse.

Acknowledgements

I would like to thank my wife, Freda, for her guidance in completing this picture book.

The sun dances in the sky.
Elle wakes up with a smile.
She wants to plant more trees in Portuana.

It's time to go to the beach.
She builds a sand castle with trees
around it.
Elle runs from the waves as she
collects seashells.

She, then, sits in a canoe to admire the changing colors of the leaves beyond the bay. She counts 7 seashells; these are well-hidden in her pouch.

It's time to sell the seashells.
At the market by the bay:
The 1st trader wants the shells
for nothing.
Elle is shrewd.
The 2nd trader wants the shells for
3 shillings.
She wants a little more.
The 3rd trader buys the seashells for
4 shillings.
Elle smiles.

12

She sits by the bay to watch the sunset beneath a canopy of trees.

It's time to go home now.
The moon is high and the tide is low.

She hears the moon whisper,
"Good night."

Elle's piggy bank is almost full now.

She dreams about life in Portuana
with more trees.

CPSIA information can be obtained
at www.ICGtesting.com
Printed in the USA
LVHW071459081020
668323LV00027B/506